PAYBACK TIME

PAYBACK TIME

Contents

Contents

PAYBACK TIME

Edgar J. Hyde

CCP

© 1997 Children's Choice Publications Ltd

Text supplied by Lesley Simpson

ISBN 1 90201 202 X

Printed and bound in UK

Chapter 1

"Is it much further now?" whinged Jodie impatiently asking for at least the fifteenth time.

"It's only a couple of miles now. Once we have passed through the town, it's only one mile to go," Mr Roper informed her.

"Now you can stop asking Jodie, we're nearly there," piped Alan, sick of listening to Jodie's moaning. Jodie stuck her tongue out at Alan and screwed her face up, quite remarkably resembling a boxer dog with no teeth.

"She's making faces at me, Mum," snitched Alan, looking at Jodie with a triumphantly smug grin on his face.

"Stop it both of you, it's not much further now," replied Mrs Roper.

Jodie and Alan normally got on well but today

was different. The overnight journey had been a long one; eleven hours. They were tired, bored and restless. Their dad, Jeff, had a new job in another town and today he and his wife, Anna, were taking them to their new home.

Alan, a very outgoing and fearless twelve year old was tall for his age with a mop of curly black hair, blue eyes and a very cheeky face with freckles speckled across his nose. He was the spitting image of his father and always ready for an adventure, the more exciting the better!

Jodie was ten and had a very pretty round face, huge green eyes and long blonde hair. The quieter of the two, she had her mother's nature. She was easily scared by her mischievous brother's pranks.

At last, rounding the final bend, the children caught their first view of the town. Heading along Main Street, Jodie and Alan looked about eagerly, taking in everything.

"There's a cinema and a Macdonalds, yipee!" Alan shouted, rubbing his hands and licking his lips at the prospect of a Big Mac in the near future.

"There's an ice rink and a huge toy shop – look over there," said Jodie pointing it out and just about losing her finger up poor Snoopy's nose.

Snoopy was a "Heinz 57" variety; a cross between a spaniel and a collie. He had a long black and white coat with long floppy black ears. He had puppy dog eyes that could charm plenty of titbits from anyone's plate, except Mum's. He was a real piece of work and very clever and he knew it.

The Post Office, Fastcash, Hairflair and Joe's Café signs grew smaller and smaller as Jodie and Alan knelt on the back seat and stared out as they left Yanihill. Friends again, their mood was charged with excitement and anticipation as they neared the final destination.

"We're here, we're here," squealed Jodie and Alan with delight as the car pulled to a halt outside their new home. Snoopy jumped about excitedly in the back of the car and barked his approval, "Woof, woof."

"Come on, boy," called Mr Roper as they all got out. Mr and Mrs Roper got some bags from the car while Jodie and Alan went to see the house.

They stared in disbelief.

"This is our new home!" Jodie mumbled trying to get over the shock. "It's a clapped out, rundown, ramshackle hovel. Mr Jones, the town tramp, back home has accommodation preferable to this and he lives in a squat!" she added.

"I think it's wicked and it's not as bad as it looks, really," Alan remarked encouragingly. "Dad will get it fixed up in no time," he added.

"Yes, I guess you're right. Race you to the door," said Jodie speeding off in the direction of the house.

No-one had lived in the house for years. An old man had lived there before but after his death the house had been neglected and had fallen into a state of disrepair. Slates were missing from the roof and the windows were boarded up making the house look sad and rejected. It stood on its own at the end of a long winding road. It was surrounded by fields and woodland making it a perfect children's paradise for adventure. And they were about to embark on the adventure of their lives!

Alan and Jodie raced up the pathway with Snoopy close on their heels, not wanting to miss out on the fun. Both children peered through the gaps in the boards trying to get their first glimpse of inside.

"I can't see anything, can you?" asked Alan.

"Not much, it's too dark but it looks kind of

spooky to me," replied Jodie.

"Come on, kids," said Mr Roper as he put down the bags and his toolbox and unlocked the door. The children charged in.

"Take it easy and be careful. Some of the floorboards are a bit loose and not very safe," warned Mr Roper.

"Okay, Dad, we'll be careful," replied Alan. They all stood in the living room in pitch black. The only light coming in was paper thin rays of sunlight that squeezed through the boards. The darkness and the shadows made the room look really eerie. It was musty and the smell of stale air and stale tobacco smoke were still very strong.

"Wow, this is like a haunted house," exclaimed Alan, his mouth hanging open with awe.

"I-i-it's cr-ee-epy, re-e-eally cr-r-eepy in here," stuttered Jodie.

"Don't be silly you two," said Mrs Roper. "Once the boards are off and the windows are open it will look different. You'll see," she added reassuringly.

"I sure hope so, Mum, because right now it reminds me of the Ghost Train ride last year at the Christmas Fair," squeaked Jodie.

"Scaredy cat," chuckled Alan.

"I am not," retorted Jodie knowing full well that her brother was right. She was a scaredy cat.

"Come on you two, and help me get the boards off and then you can really see what the house looks like," said Mrs Roper.

Mr Roper walked to the door to get the toolbox and through the glass he noticed that Snoopy had been shut out.

"Oh, you poor boy, did no one let you in!" said Mr Roper to the dog. He opened the door but Snoopy wouldn't come in.

"What is it, boy?" asked Mr Roper. "Come here, come here," he gestured slapping his legs but Snoopy wouldn't move. He growled and snarled. Something was wrong. Perhaps the Ropers didn't know it yet but Snoopy did. He knew something wasn't quite right about this house.

Mr Roper removed the boards from the windows, with the children's help, while Mrs Roper made up the picnic lunch she'd brought with them. They hadn't eaten since eight that morning when they had stopped off at a service station café. Mrs Roper knew they would be hungry soon as it was nearly twelve noon. Finishing the boards, she called them for lunch.

It was a great spread of chicken drumsticks – Alan's favourite – picnic Scotch eggs, sandwiches, sausage rolls, salad, crisps, fresh fruit salad and home-made lemonade to wash it all down. Jodie and Alan ate theirs with lightening speed; sparks almost flying from the cutlery as they wanted to explore the house in full.

"Burrrrp," belched Alan loudly, making Jodie laugh.

"Don't be rude, Alan," Mrs Roper scolded.

"Sorry! Pardon me," apologised Alan chuckling under his breath and grinning at Jodie like a Cheshire cat. "Can we go and explore now?" asked Alan.

"Yes, but be very careful. Don't be clowning around," warned Mr Roper.

"We won't," they replied and "Not!" to each other, determined to have some fun.

Chapter 2

Mrs Roper cleared away lunch and Mr Roper set to work putting the water and electricity supply on. The removal van wasn't due for another couple of hours so Mrs Roper used the time to clean up the house as best she could.

Jodie and Alan went into the house, coaxing Snoopy into tagging along with the help of some chicken scraps. Mr Roper came out of the cellar at the bottom of the staircase.

"What's down there, Dad?" asked Alan.

"It's the cellar," Mr Roper replied. "The stairs aren't too safe so don't go down there and besides there are boxes that belonged to the old man and I'll need to look through them, so stay out!" he warned.

"Oh boy, Jodie! Just the fun we're looking for

and we're not allowed. It's not fair," declared Alan. "We'll just have to sneak down there when no one's looking," he whispered to Jodie.

"Yes, let's," she replied.

In the meantime they chose to seek out adventure in another room. Snoopy growled and snarled and scratched the floor outside the closed cellar door. Jodie and Alan looked at each other bemused.

"Come on, Snoopy," called Jodie, as Alan led the way to the living room.

The living room was large with a huge open fire. There was an old grey sofa and a broken table with a lamp on it. Above the fireplace was a picture of a beautiful woman. Alan went over to get a better look, the floorboards creaking with every step. He slumped down onto the sofa. Immediately he was engulfed in a cloud of dust.

"So much for the grey sofa," he thought to himself. He couldn't see anything, or be seen. Jodie laughed at the spectacle and Alan started to sneeze.

"I wonder if that was the old man's wife," asked Jodie looking at the portrait.

"It probably was," replied Alan.

"She must have died before him. I wonder how

long he lived here on his own?" said Jodie.

"It must have been a while and he wasn't too keen on housework!" Alan remarked, still sniffing at the dust up his nose. "Or maybe he's not dead and he lives in the cellar," suggested Alan wickedly. "Maybe that's why Snoopy is acting strangely and keeps barking at the door!" Alan exclaimed giggling to himself while Jodie's face turned ashen.

"Stop it, Alan, you're frightening me. Don't tease. It's not funny," replied Jodie shaking in her shoes.

"Yes, it is funny. You always believe everything I say and I was only joking," Alan replied.

"So what if I believe you. I don't care, but this place is giving me the heebie-jeebies. There's something strange and weird about this house," added Jodie.

"I know," Alan agreed. "I'm not scared, but there is something spooky going on," he added.

"Let's go upstairs," ventured Jodie walking towards the stairs.

Alan bribed the dog into coming with the last piece of chicken. After growling and barking at the cellar door again, Snoopy was quite content to go upstairs. The stairs creaked and squeaked as they made their way to the top. Upstairs the house was light and airy. Jodie went into the first room and Alan the next.

"I'm having this room," shouted Jodie to Alan next door.

"Brilliant," replied Alan quite delighted as he wanted the room he was in.

Jodie's room was large and bright with dulling yellow wallpaper with little pink roses on it. It had a large window and a huge apple tree outside. Alan's room was a little smaller. It had a red thread-bare carpet on the floor. It also had a large window and one on the ceiling. Outside his window was a horse chestnut tree. "I'm bound to get prize winning conkers from here," he thought to himself smugly.

Bored already with their rooms, they decided to venture on through the rest of the house.

Next to Alan's room was the bathroom. It had a bath and a shower and both seemed to be in working order. At the end of the upstairs hallway was the last room. This was the largest room and would be perfect for Mum and Dad. Both Jodie and Alan were pleased as this meant that they would probably be allowed their own choice of bedroom. This bedroom looked out over the garden, which resembled an amazon jungle.

Not finding much excitement upstairs they decided to head downstairs again. Snoopy, quite at home upstairs, began to get agitated again coming towards the cellar door.

"There he goes again," remarked Jodie.

"It's probably an old cat or a mouse he can hear," Alan suggested.

"He can't hear anything, he's barking so loud."

Mrs Roper shouted to Alan and Jodie to help her in the kitchen.

"What do you want us to do?" asked Alan.

"I need you to help me clean out the cupboards and get this place scrubbed before the removal men arrive," replied Mrs Roper.

"So much for finding out what sort of cat and mouse game is going on in the cellar," Alan whispered to Jodie.

"I don't mind," said Jodie relieved.

"I know, scaredy cat," Alan teased.

Mrs Roper poured hot water into a bucket and handed them both a cloth each.

An hour on and the kitchen looked great. The

children had really worked hard and Mrs Roper was pleased.

"Come and see this," Mrs Roper called to her husband. Mr Roper was really impressed.

"It looks great. You've all done a good job here," he praised. The kitchen was big and roomy with plenty of cupboards and shelves and now that it was clean from top to bottom it was fully functional.

"Now, if the men arrive we can get the washing machine and cooker installed and I can empty all the kitchen boxes," Mrs Roper said.

"I can hear a car coming now, maybe its them," informed Alan walking to the window. "Yes it's them," he added.

"Okay, let's get going," said Mr Roper.

"Now the real fun starts," said Alan quietly to Jodie.

"What do you mean by that?" asked Jodie.

"It means, silly, that if we keep getting in the way of the men, Mum and Dad they will send us out to play. Then we will be able to sneak into the cellar," explained Alan.

"Oh, er, I don't know about that," Jodie replied with a great deal of uncertainty.

"Don't be a scaredy cat," retorted Alan.

"I'm not, well, not always, just sometimes," Jodie replied.

"Well then, prove you're not a scaredy cat now and come with me to the cellar when we get the chance," said Alan daring her.

Jodie didn't reply.

"If you don't come with me, I'll go myself and goodness knows what treasures I might uncover going through the old man's things. I won't share anything I find," he added tempting Jodie into submission. Secretly he was a little scared too, but it would be a crime to admit that to a girl, far less his sister.

"Okay, then," Jodie agreed. "But no funny stuff alright! Don't pounce out on me or anything or I'll give the game away and then we'll both be in trouble."

"Okay, it's a deal," said Alan. "Come on, I suppose we better make it look as if we are trying to help," said Alan as they left the house.

Mr and Mrs Roper were already explaining to the men what boxes should go in what rooms. Mrs Roper was a very thorough woman and liked things done properly or not at all.

She was quite a small woman with blonde hair,

blue eyes and a beautiful smile. Everyone warmed to Anna's smile. She had a very gentle nature and very rarely ever got cross with the children. Very understanding, she listened to all their problems. In practical ways, Mrs Roper was an excellent cook and a dab hand with a needle and thread.

Mr Roper was very clever with his hands. He was a Jack-of-all-Trades, but a master of none, although he did make a good job of everything he did. If anything needed mending, he'd fix it. Jeff was a very tall man with short black curly hair and blue eyes. He had a single dimple on his right cheek and when he smiled he looked far younger than his thirty-six years. He was an even tempered man but didn't stand for any nonsense. He was always ready to join in the children's games and up for an adventure at any time.

The removal men were in full swing, lugging tea chests and furniture into the house. Jodie and Alan helped as best they could with chairs and small items that didn't weigh too much. The rest of the time they spent giving oscar-winning performances of "How to mess things up without anyone finding out their hidden agenda!"

Things were going swimmingly but not fast

enough for Alan. He was very impatient and couldn't wait to get to the cellar.

"It's time for plan B," said Alan quietly to Jodie.

"What's that?" asked Jodie.

"Watch this and see," answered Alan. He walked up the ramp and into the van. He chose a small parcel and picked it up. He had to wait until someone came out of the house before he could put his plan into action. He winked at Jodie and smiled.

Just then one of the men came out of the house. Alan walked slowly down the ramp and deliberately fell off, dropping the parcel. He rolled over on the grass squealing like a pig, holding his ankle. Jodie was trying her best not to laugh at his convincing charade, and she played along.

"Mum, mum, come quickly," she shouted. "Alan has fallen and hurt his leg," she added, still trying to suppress her laughter.

The removal man looked on helplessly, not knowing what to do. Mrs Roper flew out of the house like a bullet out of a gun.

"Oh! Alan, you poor thing. Stay still or you'll make it worse," she cooed. "Where does it hurt pet, show me?" she urged.

"Ooooh! ahh, just here Mum, my ankle, my ankle, Ooooh!" Alan whined.

Mr Roper appeared and carried Alan into the house.

"I can't see anything wrong with it. You haven't broken it pet," said Mrs Roper. "I think you have just given it a bit of a turn or you have sprained it," she informed him. "Dad can put you on the couch and you can rest up there for the day," she finished, gesturing to Jeff with a nod in the direction of the living room.

"Oh! drat, I've overcooked this baby," thought Alan to himself.

"I think it's a bit better now. The pain is starting to ease off. I'll see if I can stand on it," said Alan praying his parents wouldn't twig to his prank.

He stood up and very gingerly put a little weight on his supposedly hurt leg. "Oh! it is much better," he exclaimed. "Yes, it's okay now. I'll still be able to help," he offered, knowing his mother wouldn't hear of it.

"Not so fast young man. You and Jodie have done enough for today," said Mrs Roper. "Go off and play but be careful you don't hurt your ankle again," she warned gently. "Thanks for your help, kids."

"We'll just hang about here, Mum, okay?" answered Alan.

"Whatever," came Mrs Roper's response.

"Brilliant," said Alan. "Wasn't I brilliant?" he asked smugly.

"Yeah, but you nearly blew it," said Jodie.

"Right, let's get Snoopy and hover about inside and when the coast is clear we can sneak down to the cellar," said Alan taking charge of the situation.

Snoopy was nosing around outside and watching eagerly at the comings and goings.

"There he is," said Jodie. "Snoopy, here, boy!"

Snoopy came bounding over and Jodie scooped him up under her arm. Reaching the steps outside the house she turned to Alan and asked in a whisper, "What if he starts barking at the door again?"

"Put your hand around his snout and keep his trap shut," said Alan getting impatient. "Now let's go," he commanded.

"Yes, sir," she said, sticking her tongue out behind his back. He can be so bossy, she thought to herself.

As luck would have it nobody was about so they made a dash for the door. It's now or never, Jodie thought to herself. Her heart was pounding madly; it was beating so fast and loud she was sure Alan would be able to hear it. I am scared. Why am I doing this? she asked herself, not knowing what the answer was. It was too late to turn back now.

The handle turned with ease and they both entered the cellar. Snoopy made a small whining sound but not loud enough to draw attention to himself.

"Shh!" said Jodie quietening the dog. "Where's the light switch, Alan?" she asked in a whisper.

"I don't know," replied Alan. They both groped around feeling the walls.

"I've got it," said Alan switching it on.

"That's better," said Jodie. "Now I can see and so can Snoopy. If there are any ghouls or ugly hobgoblins down here he'll see them first and sound the alarm."

"Don't be silly Jodie, and be quiet," said Alan.

"Maybe he won't bark if I let go his jaws now," said Jodie.

"Not yet, he'll give us away if he does bark," replied Alan.

That's what I was hoping for, thought Jodie wanting to back out.

The staircase was long and very steep and some of the steps did look a little suspect.

"Let's go slowly. Follow me and put your feet the same places as I do," ordered Alan. "I'll test them first to see if they're alright."

Very slowly they made their way down the stairs. Halfway down and they could see into the cellar. "Wow! Look at all the boxes and chests in here," exclaimed Alan.

"Yes, this is fantastic," admitted Jodie, her confidence growing with every step. The anticipation of what goodies lay in store inside the boxes now far outweighed her fear.

The cellar was enormous. Pipes ran along the ceiling and up the walls and they were covered in a multitude of spiders' webs. There were wires and cables everywhere, going in all different directions. Boxes were piled high in rows and rows, with at least an inch of dust on them. On one wall there was a set of shelves with large glass jars on them. Some contained coloured liquid, others were full of pickled onions which looked like rotting eyeballs.

"Jodie, look at all those jars over there," said Alan pointing them out.

"Eeh! yuck! What's in them?" asked Jodie.

"I don't know," said Alan. "Maybe it's Dr

Jekyll's laboratory!" he suggested wickedly.

"No, it's not," retorted Jodie and went on to ask, "Who is Dr Jekyll?"

"Oh, nobody," answered Alan, realising if she had known who Dr Jekyll was she could get scared again and spoil everything.

In the corner under the stairs there was a large boiler and next to that there was an old furnace. Across on the other side of the room there was an electric saw.

"Hey Jodie, check out the saw," said Alan.

"Dad can use that to cut up the wood for the floorboards," Jodie replied. "Can I put Snoopy down now?" she asked. "My arm is killing me. He hasn't made a sound in ages," she added.

"I suppose you can give it a try but don't put him down, just let go of his mouth and see if he barks. Be ready to gag him again if he does," said Alan.

Jodie slowly let go of Snoopy's jaws, ever ready to snap them shut again if he so much as made a whimper. Snoopy didn't bark.

"Good boy," said Jodie praising him.

"Good boy, clever boy," said Alan relieved that he hadn't given the game away. "I think it's safe to put him down now," Alan remarked.

"Okay, here goes," said Jodie setting him down. Snoopy ran over to the corner of the room and sat down in front of an old easy chair, that had seen better days and started wagging his tail. The chair looked as if it had exploded. The upholstery was ripped and the stuffing was bulging out from all angles.

"What's Snoopy up to?" asked Alan bemused.

"I'm sure I don't know," replied Jodie. "You're the smarty pants in this family, so you tell me!"

"Well, er, maybe there's a family of mice nesting inside the chair. It's not fit for anything else," exclaimed Alan. "Snoopy seems happy enough over there so let's go and have a proper nose around," he suggested.

"Hey, Alan come and see this," said Jodie walking towards a screened off window. "Look, I bet this opens," said Jodie. "If we can manage to open it and close it we could use it as a secret entrance and we can come and go as often as we please without anyone knowing," stated Jodie pleased as punch that she had made the discovery. "Give me a hand with it."

"The hinges don't look up to much, so we'll have to be careful," said Alan. They pushed and pulled and slowly the window started to slacken.

"That's it, keep going," said Alan. "A little more, a bit more. Yes, we've done it. Go and get that crate, over there," ordered Alan, holding the window up and peering out. Jodie dragged the crate across the floor. "Shh!" said Alan, "they"ll hear us," he warned.

"Well give me a hand then and we can lift it," Jodie replied.

"Let's set it down here and we can use it as a step to climb in and out," said Alan. "Hold the window up while I get out," he added.

"Don't stand up when you get out there, if there's a window above us and we're seen, we are rumbled for sure," said Jodie.

"I'm not stupid, Jodie," retorted Alan hotly.

"Okay, okay, what can you see?" asked Jodie as Alan climbed out the window and crawled on his tummy.

"There isn't a window above us but the back door is a little further along, but it's cool. There's a big wooden bunker with logs in it, that will hide us going in and out," Alan informed her.

"Great. Now come on back," she said, not wanting to be left on her own in the cellar.

Alan climbed in backwards and put his feet on the crate. "That was a breeze," he said making it look easy. "Now, let's get to those boxes," suggested Alan.

Snoopy was lying on the chair quite happily as Alan and Jodie carefully took down a box from the pile.

"Open it, open it!" said Jodie excitedly.

They opened the box and peered in. On the top was a layer of books. "This isn't very exciting," said Jodie deflated at their find.

"It can't all be books, silly. It would be too heavy for us to lift. Let's pile them up on the floor," suggested Alan.

Little Women, A Tale of Two Cities, War and Peace, Jane Eyre, The Mill on the Floss, Treasure Island amongst others were gradually being piled up on the floor.

"Ah! see, I told you it wasn't all books!" exclaimed Alan uncovering the goodies beneath. There were some framed pictures and an old rusty tin.

"Now, this looks interesting," said Alan lifting up the tin and giving it a shake. It rattled. Opening it, Alan's eyes grew wide and he stared at the contents.

"Wowee!" he exclaimed "Look at these medals," said Alan showing Jodie.

"They're beautiful," said Jodie, "do you think they are real gold?"

"I don't know but they look pretty good to me," answered Alan. "Go and get that crate from under the stairs and the old blanket lying on the saw bench."

Carefully Alan and Jodie took the medals out of the box one by one and laid them out on their make-shift table.

"The old man must have been very brave to have been decorated with all these medals," said Jodie dazzled by their find.

"This one's a cross," said Alan.

"This one's a star, it's my favourite so far," said Jodie taking it from the tin. "They are so shiny they look almost brand new."

"I bet the old man polished these every day. He must have been really proud of them," stated Alan admiring the man for being such a brave soldier.

"How many are there?" asked Jodie as Alan took the last one out and laid it down.

"There's fifteen," counted Alan.

"Now, that's amazing," said Jodie in awe. "Are they worth any money, do you think?"

"They could be," replied Alan. "They are very

old and in good condition and some of them are from the World War I. Lots of people collect them," he added. "We better put them back now."

Next, Jodie found a photograph album.

"Look at these, Alan," said Jodie holding out the album for Alan to see. "I think the first one must be the old man when he was young. He looks nice," added Jodie pointing him out.

"Yes," replied Alan, giggling, "but look at his bandy legs. He looks as if his horse has bolted," he joked, unable to suppress his laughter. Jodie burst out laughing as well.

"Shh!" said Jodie realising they were making too much noise. "We shouldn't laugh at him," she said feeling guilty, "I didn't like it when everyone at school laughed at my braces."

"That was ages ago and you only had to wear them for a couple of weeks, it was nothing," said Alan.

"Well, it wasn't nothing to me. No one would play with me if it was a cloudy day just in case a freak bolt of lightening struck me and they got electrocuted as well. No one would let me play tig after Susie Cook's hair got trapped in them. They called me Jaws, after that big man in the James Bond film, and metal mouth. The old woman next door, the one that laughed like a witch, she told me that every time I walked passed her house I interfered with her television reception and she made me walk the long way round to the shops," finished Jodie feeling sure now that Alan would remember just how bad it had been for her.

"I'm sorry, Jaw– I mean, Jodie," said Alan laughing. "Really, Jodie, I am sorry and I never teased you," he added.

"No, you didn't," replied Jodie, knowing he wasn't such a bad brother.

"There's the woman who is in the portrait upstairs," said Alan, his attention back on the album and not on trying to keep a straight face listening to Jodie's heart wrenching tale of woe!

"So it is and I guess those must be their children. I wonder where they are now?" Jodie asked.

"They're probably dead as well and if not they must be reaching fossilisation," Alan replied, giggling. The rest of the album contained pictures of family gatherings and the old man's army days.

Bored with the pictures they turned their attention to the box again.

Alan found the old man's army uniform. "Phew, it's a bit wiffy," said Alan screwing up his face.

"It can't be that bad if you're putting it on," said Jodie watching him as he fastened the buttons.

"Pass me the hat," said Alan. Turning to Jodie, Alan asked "How do I look?"

He marched to the far end of the cellar, stopping and saluting the walls. "You look stupid," answered Jodie laughing at his antics.

"No, YOU DON'T," came a voice from the corner where Snoopy was lying. Alan looked over and back at Jodie.

"What did you say?" he asked her.

"I said you looked stupid," she replied.

"I know that but what did you say after that," he went on.

"I didn't say anything," replied Jodie.

"Yes, you did," he demanded.

"No, I didn't," protested Jodie. "I know what I said!" she added hotly, annoyed that he didn't believe her. Taking her head out of the box she looked at Alan. "Why?" she asked.

Alan's face was as white as a sheet and he was

visibly shaking from head to foot.

"What's wrong?" she asked.

"I h-h-heard a v-v-voice, s-s-someone sp-sp-spoke to me. They s-s-said, 'No you don't'," he stammered his blood running cold and the hairs on his back standing on end.

"I didn't hear anything," Jodie stated. "Oh, I get it, stop it, Alan, I know what you are doing and it won't work. You're not going to scare me. Nice try though," she added.

"I'm not pretending, Jodie. Let's get out of here. This place is giving me the willies," said Alan tearing at the buttons in blind panic.

He threw the uniform and the hat and the books, everything on the floor into the box.

"Hurry up and help me," said Alan. They replaced the box on the pile.

Jodie sensed that Alan was telling the truth. She was now quite scared but still couldn't be sure that he wasn't joking. After all she hadn't heard the voice.

"Grab Snoopy and we'll get out the escape hatch," said Alan making a dash for it. Jodie grabbed Snoopy and headed for the window just in time to see Alan disappear through it.

"Wait for me," wailed Jodie after him.

She opened the hatch and threw Snoopy out as if launching him into space and scrambled out after him. Jodie chased after Alan until he stopped at the end of the garden. His heart was pounding and he was scared witless.

"Are you joking with me, Alan? Tell the truth!"

"I swear, Jodie, I heard a voice," said Alan trying to convince Jodie that he hadn't made it up. He knew that if Jodie had believed him, really believed him, she would have brought the house down with her screams.

"Maybe it was the men outside you heard or maybe Dad," urged Jodie. "The voice might not have been talking to you and don't forget, I didn't hear it. I was in the room with you and I didn't hear it!" she said trying to make sense of it all. There had to be a simple explanation. There just had to be, she thought.

Alan began to calm down. Perhaps she's right, he thought, starting to doubt his own mind.

"Do you want to go back in and find out?" asked Jodie.

"No," said Alan "I think I'd like to play out here for a while. I've had enough excitement for today.'

"Wait for me," wailed Jodie after him.

She opened the hatch and threw Snoopy out as if launching him into space and scrambled out after him. Jodie chased after Alan until he stopped at the end of the garden. His heart was pounding and he was scared witless.

"Are you joking with me, Alan? Tell the truth."

"I swear, Jodie, I heard a voice," said Alan trying to convince Jodie that he hadn't made it up. He knew that if Jodie had believed him, really believed him, she would have brought the house down with her screams.

"Maybe it was the men outside you heard or maybe Dad," urged Jodie. "The voice might not have been talking to you and don't forget I didn't hear it. I was in the room with you and I didn't hear it," she said trying to make sense of it all. There had to be a simple explanation. There just had to be, she thought.

Alan began to calm down. Perhaps she's right, he thought, starting to doubt his own mind.

"Do you want to go back in and find out?" asked Jodie.

"No," said Alan. "I think I'd like to play out here for a while. I've had enough excitement for today.

Chapter 3

The removal men were ready to leave. The last box was taken into the house and the other man removed the ramp. Mr and Mrs Roper paid and thanked the men for a job well done.

"Well, that's that done," said Mr Roper, "but we still have plenty to do inside," he added.

"I know, but most of the things that need doing today are done now," said Mrs Roper quite pleased that she had everything under control. "I've cleaned the children's bedrooms and their beds are made up. They can give me a hand putting their clothes away and tomorrow we can arrange things better and they can put their posters up. It will have to do until we decorate and that will be a while off yet, judging by the cost that the repairs for the house will add up to."

"Tomorrow we'll all go into town and I'll go to the bank and the builders yard and order what I need," said Mr Roper. "While I'm doing that you can take the kids to Macdonalds for lunch if you like," he suggested.

"Whatever you say, dearest," Mrs Roper teased, smiling up at her husband. "Come on, back to work," she coaxed, dragging Mr Roper by the arm. "I've got to make our bed up or we'll be sleeping on the floor!" she laughed, walking into the house.

Mr Roper carried on where he'd left off, measuring this and that and jotting it all down in his notebook. Mrs Roper checked on dinner and went upstairs.

"Alan, Jodie, dinner," shouted Mrs Roper out the back door.

"They can't have realised the time," said Mrs Roper to her husband.

"They'll be having too much fun to be thinking of their stomachs," replied Mr Roper setting the table. "They won't be far and if they didn't hear us, Snoopy would," laughed Mr Roper knowing that Snoopy could hear the grass growing under his feet.

Mr and Mrs Roper started their meal and before

40

long Alan and Jodie came bursting in followed closely by Snoopy.

"Hi, have you had fun?" asked Mrs Roper.

"Er, yeah, too much," said Alan looking sideways at Jodie and winking.

"I'm starving," said Jodie, her stomach rumbling its approval.

"I'm not surprised," said Mr Roper "you've been away for hours. So tell us, what did you get up to?"

"We played on the swing in the garden and then we took Snoopy for a walk," said Jodie.

"We found a river and it looks as if it would be worth getting the rods out. We saw some fish in the shallows but they were pretty small. Perhaps there will be bigger ones in the deeper water," said Alan.

"Once we've settled in we can give it a try," replied Mr Roper.

"Can we do it at night again with the lamps and the midnight feast?" asked Alan.

"Yes, of course we can," said Mr Roper.

"Can I come too?" asked Jodie.

"Yes, the more the merrier," Mr Roper answered.

"Eat up, kids," said Mrs Roper. "Once Dad's

finished his dinner he's going to set up the television and you can watch it for an hour and then it's off to bed. It's been a long hard day for all of us and we could all use an early night."

The childen didn't raise any arguments; they were tired after their adventure in the cellar.

Snoopy having scoffed his dinner sat at the end of the table hoping for some welcome titbits. He was suitably rewarded with a chunk of meat from Alan's plate. Two chews and it was gone. Alan always cut off the meat that had fat on it and Snoopy knew this. Alan slipped another piece to Snoopy but this time he was caught.

"Don't encourage the dog to beg for scraps, Alan," Mrs Roper scolded. "Save the pieces and put them in his dish."

"Sorry," apologised Alan, not really sorry because it was more fun this way. If there was anything Alan didn't like on his plate his four legged waste disposal machine always came in handy!

"That was great, Mum," said Jodie appreciatively. "What's for pudding?" she asked.

"Apple pie and cream," she replied grinning at her daughter, as it was her favourite.

Mr Roper skipped pudding, to Jodie's delight as there would be more for her, and went to set up the television. The children gulped down their dessert and went off to watch television, leaving Mum to do the dishes, as usual.

"Right kids, time's up," said Mrs Roper. "Get washed and brush your teeth. Your pyjamas are on your beds and when you're ready I'll tuck you in."

The children raced upstairs and went to their rooms. They got ready for bed. Alan made it to the bathroom first and then Jodie.

"Good night, Alan," Jodie called from her room.

"Good night, Jodie," Alan called from his room.

"Good night ,you pair," said Mr Roper standing in between the two doors, laughing. "See you in the morning – sweet dreams."

Mrs Roper tucked them in and kissed them good night. "God Bless," she said, as she did every night.

Chapter 4

Dawn broke and Mr and Mrs Roper rose early. So much still had to be done, especially as Mr Roper would be starting his new job in four weeks, leaving him little spare time to fix up the house.

They left the children sleeping and went down to have breakfast. Mrs Roper prepared eggs, bacon, mushrooms and fried tomato with a few rounds of toast and a large pot of tea.

"Here he comes, right on cue," said Mrs Roper hearing Snoopy's paws on the wooden stairs. His footsteps stopped but he didn't come into the kitchen.

"That's strange," said Mr Roper. "When Snoopy smells food you can count on him being here."

"Go and take a look Jeff," said Mrs Roper.

He found Snoopy sitting at the cellar door wagging his tail.

"He's a strange one," he said walking back to the kitchen. "He never passes up a meal but today he'd rather sit at the cellar door."

"He was acting strange yesterday, remember. He was growling and snarling and scratching the floor. Perhaps you should go and see what's down there that has him so distracted.

"We'll both take a look, come on," said Mr Roper.

Mr Roper opened the cellar door and Snoopy bounded down the stairs.

"There must be a cat or something he's after," said Mr Roper putting on the light and following Snoopy. "Just watch the steps, Anna."

They saw Snoopy lying on the moth-eaten chair, wagging his tail quite contentedly.

"Oh well, I guess he just likes being down here," said Mrs Roper going back upstairs.

They finished breakfast and planned their day.

The first stop for Mr Roper was the bank. He needed a loan to help pay for the work to be done on the house and for all the materials he would use. He was worried that the bank might not lend him the money that he needed, because he was a new customer. Mr Roper was having to open a new account at a new bank as there wasn't a branch of his own bank in Yanihill. Their second stop would be the shops and then on to the builder's yard.

Mrs Roper heard soft footsteps on the stairs.

"Good morning, sweetie," she said, greeting her daughter warmly.

"Morning," croaked Jodie still tired.

"You're up early," said Mrs Roper. "It's only seven o'clock."

"The sun was shining in the window and it woke me."

"Perhaps tomorrow that won't be a problem," said Mr Roper. "We're going shopping today and we'll get blinds for the bedroom windows.

"Can I chose mine?" asked Jodie.

"Yes, and a little later on you can pick your wallpaper as well," said Mrs Roper.

Another set of footsteps brought Alan downstairs. "Good morning, sweetie. Did the sun waken you as well?" asked Mrs Roper.

"Yes," replied Alan. "Where's Snoopy? He wasn't in his basket when I got up."

"He's downstairs in the cellar," replied Mr

Roper. Alan was instantly wide awake.

"Go and fetch him," said Mrs Roper chopping up his meat.

Alan scowled at Jodie not knowing what to do. He was still scared after yesterday but didn't want his parents to know that they had been down there.

"That's not a good idea," said Mr Roper. "The stairs aren't safe. I'll get him," he said walking out the kitchen.

"Whew!" thought Alan to himself and smiled at Jodie. Dad had saved the day!

The children had breakfast and played outside until it was time to go to Yanihill. Everyone piled into the car and they drove off. Jodie and Alan were excited at the prospect of all the new shops and finding out more about the entertainment that was on offer.

"What's that funny smell?" asked Jodie as they neared the town. "Is there a farm near here? Yuck! It's getting stronger!" she exclaimed.

"I can smell it too," said Alan holding his nose tightly, Jodie following suit. The acrid stench filtered through to the front of the car.

"Boy, oh, boy! Snoopy. Thanks a lot," said Mr Roper, looking round at the dog sitting proudly on the seat. Hastily they all rolled down the windows in order to rid the car of the pungent odour that only Snoopy could call his own.

"What are you feeding him on, Anna – toxic waste!" remarked Mr Roper.

"Aw, poor Snoopy. It was probably the long journey yesterday that's upset his stomach. It's not his fault," said Mrs Roper defending the dog.

"He's not sleeping in my room any more," stated Alan. "It's the first and last time he'll launch a rancid attack on my sense of smell."

"Where's the best place to park, do you think?" asked Mrs Roper.

"We can drive along a bit and see what we can find," replied Mr Roper.

"Over there's perfect," said Mrs Roper pointing to the supermarket car park.

Mr Roper headed off to the bank while Mrs Roper and the children went shopping. They would meet up back at the car in an hour.

Mr Roper's appointment at the bank was swift. He didn't get the loan. He didn't know what he was going to do as he needed the materials to fix the house straight away. On his way back to the car he noticed a large yellow sign that read Fastcash. I suppose it's worth a look, he thought, not having much choice.

The small sign on the window offered any cash sum, with good interest rates. Mr Roper entered the shop and saw a wily looking man in his late thirties. He had short red hair and deep set piggy eyes, too close together, topped with bushy red eyebrows in complete disarray. His mouth was thin, in fact so thin he hardly had any lips at all. He looks like Basil Brush, he thought and then smirked to himself realising that Basil Brush was better looking.

The man was busy and he gestured to Mr Roper to take a seat and wait. He moved about furtively from the desk to the filing cabinet and then to the 'phone. His transaction completed he replaced the receiver and filed away some documents.

"Good morning, Sir, how can I help you?" asked the man smiling, and displaying saffron coloured teeth that looked no better than a row of condemned houses.

He really is an unfortunate looking character, Mr Roper thought. "Yes, I would like some information about getting a loan," said Mr Roper.

"Fine, fine. William Robb's the name," said the

man, offering Mr Roper his hand. "Will to my friends."

"Jeff Roper," said Mr Roper and they shook hands.

"Please come through to my office," said Mr Robb ushering Mr Roper into the office. "Please take a seat – take two if you like – just my little joke, ha, ha."

"Oh, er, yes, huh huh." Mr Roper feigned laughter at the man's sad attempt at humour.

The men spoke for a while and William Robb gave Mr Roper all the information he needed. Mr Roper was satisfied that although he would be paying back slightly more than he would at the bank, the rates were reasonable and well within his budget. The arrangements were made, the document signed and the money changed hands. Mr Roper could relax now as he had the money to finish fixing the house. Mr Roper walked back to the car, stepping lightly on his feet with not a care in the world.

On reaching the car he discovered that Mrs Roper and the children had been back and left the groceries in the car. There was a note stuck to the steering wheel which read "Gone to the textile store, next to the newsagents; get you in there."

Jodie had already picked her blinds but Alan was undecided.

"Why don't you toss a coin," suggested Jodie trying to help. "Or you can ask Dad, here he comes," she added moving over to him.

Mr Roper and Alan had a man-to-man talk and Alan finally made his choice.

"How did it go at the bank, Jeff?" asked Mrs Roper quietly.

"It didn't," he replied flatly.

"What are we going to do?"

"I've got it all under control," he replied smiling smugly at his wife.

"Oh yes! Do tell," urged Mrs Roper wanting to know what he meant.

"We've got the money and I'll explain later. Now, if you're all done here, we can go to the builders' yard," said Mr Roper. "It's too early for lunch yet."

The Ropers went back to the car and drove to the builders' yard. It was huge. There was everything one could possibly imagine that was needed to build a house. There were pallets of differently coloured bricks stacked high. There was gravel, cement, sand, metal girders, timber of all sizes, lengths and colours.

"This place is amazing," said Alan to Jodie. "Dad could build us a tree house if we're really good and we nag him constantly. Everything he'll need is here," he added.

"I'd love a tree house," Jodie agreed. "Dad, could you build us a tree house, please?" she pleaded.

"First things first. Once the house is finished we'll see," Mr Roper replied walking towards an assistant.

Mr Roper ordered his materials and paid the bill. "It will all be delivered tomorrow morning," assured the assistant moving on to his next customer.

"Lunch time," announced Mr Roper. "Anna, you take the kids to Macdonalds and order the food. I'll get something from that snack bar and we'll take Snoopy to the park and eat there."

They finished their lunch, walked back to the car and went home.

Mrs Roper put the groceries away and Jodie and Alan went out to play with Snoopy. Mr Roper, with the help of his wife, took the saw and bench outside. He lifted some of the damaged floorboards and cut off the good bits so he could mend the cellar stairs.

The rest of the day passed uneventfully for Jodie and Alan, little knowing what would be lying in store for them the next day.

Chapter 5

The bricks from the builders' yard arrived next morning and Jodie and Alan helped their dad unload the materials at the back door beside the saw. Snoopy sat beside the escape hatch wagging his tail, wanting to go into the cellar.

After lunch the children were bored. The sound of hammering and banging filled the house. Then, there would be silence and the saw would start up outside.

"Come on Jodie, think," said Allan trying to come up with ideas of what they could do.

"I want to have a rummage through the boxes in the cellar but you are too scared," said Jodie.

"I'm not," answered Alan. "It probably was just my imagination," he added, but secretly still a bit scared. "Okay, we'll go to the cellar." he agreed.

"Next time Dad uses the saw we'll wait until he has finished and then sneak in through the hatch," suggested Jodie going to the back of the house and seeing Snoopy was still there.

Mr Roper cut some wood and went into the house through the back door.

"Right, the coast is clear," said Alan dashing towards the hatch.

Alan dropped Snoopy onto the crate and one at a time they climbed in backwards.

"It's so dark," said Jodie. "Go and put the light on, Alan," said Jodie, too scared to do it herself.

"No, you do it," he replied, refusing point blank.

"We'll both go then," suggested Jodie.

They fumbled their way blindly to the staircase and Alan went up and put the light on. Jodie looked around and saw that, apart from the saw being missing, everything was as they had left it.

"Let's get the same box down," said Jodie. "I saw a jewellery box at the bottom of it," she added.

They opened the box and sure enough, underneath everything was an old wooden jewellery box.

Jodie opened the box, her eyes wide in amazement. "Wow!" she exclaimed. "Get a look at these," she said to Alan, her eyes not leaving the jewels.

Most of it was costume jewellery but to Jodie it was like looking at the Crown Jewels.

"Look at these diamonds," she said, holding up a necklace.

"They won't be diamonds," said Alan "just glass."

"They're still beautiful," replied Jodie.

"I like this," said Alan taking a man's pocket watch and chain out of the box.

"A locket!" exclaimed Jodie. "Here's a locket," she went on. "I've always wanted one."

It was a gold locket in the shape of a heart. Jodie opened it and on one side there was a picture of the old man and on the other his wife.

"I wish I could keep it," said Jodie putting the chain over her head and looking down at it admiringly.

"THAT WOULD BE STEALING," came the voice from the corner where the chair was.

Jodie was rigid, frozen stiff. Her jeans grew darker as the warm liquid ran down her legs. "Ahhh!" screamed Jodie, drowned out by the saw.

"What is it Jodie?" asked Alan in a panic.

"It-it's the voice," stammered Jodie.

"I can't hear it," said Alan watching Jodie, who could now move, making a dash for the escape hatch.

"Don't go!" came the voice again. "Don't be scared, I won't hurt you," he said.

Alan grabbed Jodie before she reached the window. "You can't go out now. We'll get caught and Dad will kill us," said Alan, blocking her way.

Jodie was petrified and couldn't think straight.

"Tell your brother to put the silver ring on," came the voice. Jodie started crying.

"The voice said you have to put a silver ring on," she sobbed knowing they were trapped and would have to live through this nightmare. "He said he won't hurt us," she added.

"I won't Jodie, I promise," said the voice reassuringly.

Jodie was numb. She didn't understand what was happening. Alan grabbed the box and scrabbled through it until he found the ring and put it on.

"Can you hear me now, Alan?" said the voice.

"Y-y-yes," Alan replied.

"Don't go, please. I need your help," said the voice.

"Who are you, or what are you?" asked Alan trembling.

"I'm Albert. You can call me uncle Albert. I lived in this house before I died," he answered. "I am a ghost but you mustn't be scared," he added. "Snoopy, your dog is my friend now. He knows I'm not evil. Animals can sense when something is wrong or bad," said Albert convincing the children that he was a good ghost. "I'm sorry I frightened you yesterday and again now," apologised Albert.

"Why didn't I hear you yesterday and why didn't Alan hear you just then?" asked Jodie very confused but not so scared.

"Only when you are wearing a personal possession of mine or my wife's will you be able to hear me."

Now it made sense to Jodie and Alan.

"If you like, you can see me too," offered Albert.

"How can we do that?" asked Alan.

"You have to own and wear something that once belonged to us," Albert informed them.

"We don't have any money to buy anything," said Jodie growing evermore confident.

"That's easily taken care of. Alan, keep the ring,

it's a gift and Jodie, you may keep the locket."

No sooner had he finished speaking when he became visible. He was sitting in the chair with Snoopy on his knee.

"Jeepers creepers!" said Alan in amazement.

"This is incredible!" said Jodie.

Albert now had tufty white hair and skin that resembled walnut shells. Apart from that he didn't look much different than his photograph, only older.

"Hello, Uncle Albert, I'm Jodie," she said introducing herself, "and this is Alan."

"Hello," said Alan.

"I'm very pleased to meet you both," replied Albert smiling broadly.

"Nobody is going to believe this when we tell them," stated Alan.

"Oh, no! You mustn't tell anyone about me. It must be our secret. Do you both promise?" asked Albert waiting for their reply.

"Cross my heart and hope to die," said Jodie. "Oh, sorry. I didn't mean that," she added, realising her badly chosen phrase. "I promise," she said.

"I promise too," said Alan smirking at Jodie's blunder.

"Why are you a ghost?" asked Jodie. "Why didn't you go to heaven or wherever it is you go to when you die?"

"Sometimes, if something goes wrong or is left unfinished, you are left in a ghostly state until you can put things right and then you leave this world forever."

"So why didn't you leave this world. Why are you still here?" asked Jodie.

"Don't be nosy," said Alan also wanting to know but not wanting to be rude.

"That's alright, little one," said Albert winking at Jodie. "My wife, Mary and our two children, Andrew and Lucy, were killed in an accident. I didn't have any money to pay for their funerals so I borrowed money from a loan company in town. These men turned out to be very evil. They increased my payments and charged me more and more money every time I saw them. It ended up I was going to have to pay them more than twice the sum I had borrowed. When I couldn't pay them they beat me up. This happened several times before I died. It was the same men that found me and didn't tell anyone. I was dead for a week before anybody found me."

"That's awful," said Jodie, upset by his story.

"My unfinished business is to stop these evil men and drive them out of town for good."

"Why didn't you go to the police?" asked Alan.

"The men were not breaking the law," replied Albert, "the contract that I signed to borrow the money had a lot of small print and I didn't bother reading it. It turned out that the men were allowed to raise their interest rate whenever they wanted. When they beat me up there were no witnesses and it was their word against mine. That's why I didn't go to the police," finished Albert.

"Is this why you asked for our help?" asked Alan.

"Yes," said Albert.

"What can we do?" asked Jodie wanting to help so the evil men would get their just desserts.

"I'm not quite sure yet but I wouldn't put you in any danger," replied Albert reassuring them. "I'll think of something but in the meantime you had better run along. Come and see me tomorrow," invited Albert.

Jodie and Alan put away the box and thanked Albert for their presents.

"We'd better hide our gifts or Mum and Dad will know we have been in here and they will think we have stolen them," said Alan taking his ring off and putting it in his pocket.

Jodie took off her locket and noticed that Albert was invisible again. She ran up the stairs and switched off the light. They could hear Mr Roper hammering inside the house so they made their getaway unnoticed.

"Jodie, what happened to you?" asked Mrs Roper looking at her wet trousers.

"We were playing too far away and I couldn't make it back in time," she lied.

"I'll run you a bath," said Mrs Roper heading upstairs. "You can have one, too," she called back to Alan. "Dad's taking us to see *The Lost World* at the cinema tonight."

"Yippee!" squealed Alan in delight.

"Excellent," said Jodie trying to walk without her trousers rubbing.

Jodie and Alan lay awake that night reliving the best bits of the film in their minds and wishing it was already morning so they could go and see Albert again.

Chapter 6

Washed, fed and watered the children took their earliest opportunity to go and see uncle Albert. This was the routine every morning now and they had only been at the new house a week. The hammering, banging and sawing still continued as Mr Roper fixed up the house. He was making a really good job it, helped by the fact that the children kept out of his way. This wasn't a problem for the kids as they spent the best part of the day hidden away in the cellar, learning all about Albert and his wife.

Without warning the cellar door opened.

"I must have left the light on," said Mr Roper to himself.

Jodie and Alan heard him and squeezed behind the boiler to hide. Mr Roper came downstairs to get another box of nails. As he left he switched the light off.

"That was a close shave," said Alan to Jodie coming out from behind the boiler.

"Yes, it was," replied Jodie, tiptoeing upstairs to put the light back on.

Halfway up, she heard the 'phone ringing.

"It's a Mr William Robb for you," Mrs Roper shouted to her husband.

"Coming," he replied. "What do you mean I'm a day late with the payment? It says the sixteenth on the card," he said angrily. "No, no, don't bother, I'm on my way to see you now," said Mr Roper slamming the receiver down.

"What was that about?" Mrs Roper asked, concerned that her husband was so angry.

"I don't believe it, Mr Robb, the man I got the loan from said I should have made a payment yesterday and because I'm late I've to pay double. It's an outrage and I'm going to sort this man out right now," he said picking the car keys up from the table.

"Be careful," said Mrs Roper realising there could be trouble.

"I'll be fine," Mr Roper replied going out the

front door.

Switching on the light Jodie went back downstairs to tell Albert and Alan what she had heard.

"Did you say Mr William Robb?" asked Albert, praying that it wouldn't be.

"Yes, William Robb. He told Dad he was late in paying and he's to pay double. Dad's just left in the car to go and see him," she finished.

"Oh, no," said Albert shaking his head. "That's the man I borrowed money from. He changes the rules to get more money out of people *and* he's a thug. I just hope your father will be alright," said Albert. "He's going to need help and I intend to stop those men once and for all," he said trying to think of a plan.

Mr Roper arrived at the Fastcash office, blazing.

"Ah, Mr Roper, please come through," said Mr Robb going into his small office. Sitting behind the desk was another man. He was fat.

"This is my brother, Sid," said Mr Robb introducing them.

Sid had dark tufty hair like a wired-haired terrier. He also had piggy little eyes, a very fat face that sagged and big rubbery lips. He bore an uncanny resemblance to a bloodhound. Sid smiled at Mr Roper revealing teeth that could only be described as a dentist's nightmare.

"Now then, let's get this little matter cleared up," said Sid in a gruff voice.

"Yes, let's," replied Mr Roper angrily.

"You should have paid us yesterday," said Sid smugly. "Because you have defaulted, we charge a nominal fee. It's in the contract," he added.

"A nominal fee! You're charging me double what I owe you. This is an outrage!" shouted Mr Roper barely in control of his temper.

"Oh, I wouldn't say that," said Will. "We were good enough to lend you some money when the bank wouldn't. I think you are being very ungrateful."

"Ungrateful," repeated Mr Roper. "You are loan sharks. I don't know why I didn't realise it before. You are crooks, thieves and I'm not going to pay it," he finished.

"I don't think that's a very good idea," said Sid getting out of his chair and walking towards Mr Roper, towering over him. "We have ways of making you pay," he added, grabbing Mr Roper's arm and twisting it up his back.

"Okay, okay, let go," said Mr Roper in agony.

Sid was very strong and menacing. He let Mr Roper go, giving him a chance to stand up. Then without warning Sid punched Mr Roper in the face, sending him flying backwards. Will caught him, spun him round and punched him in the stomach. Mr Roper lashed out at Will but was grabbed from behind by his hair. Sid dragged Mr Roper to the ground and kicked him repeatedly until Mr Roper, rolled up like a ball, begged them to stop.

"Now then, Mr Roper, I think you understand it now, don't you," said Sid, helping Mr Roper to his feet and giving him a hanky. Mr Roper held the hanky to his nose to try and stop the bleeding. He fumbled about in his pocket for his wallet. He paid the money knowing he was beaten.

"I'll get you for this I swear I will," said Mr Roper threatening the men.

"Oh, no you won't," said Sid laughing evily at Mr Roper. "It's us that has got you. You signed on the dotted line," he added roaring with laughter as Mr Roper turned to leave the office.

"Just one more thing," said Will. "Because of the trouble you have given us we are adding ten percent onto each of your payments. That's in the contract too," he laughed, waving Mr Roper off.

Mr Roper went back to his car furious and feeling very sore and cleaned himself up. His nose was very swollen, like a ripe tomato.

"What will Anna think about it all?" thought Mr Roper.

He was in trouble and he knew it. As soon as his money was sorted out back home and transferred to his new bank he would pay off these evil men in full.

Hearing the car return, Jodie and Alan went up to the cellar door and listened to Dad tell Mum the terrible story.

"They punched him and beat him," said Alan in horror to Albert.

"And they've added ten percent to every one of his payments," exclaimed Jodie not understanding what it really meant.

"Why did he borrow money from those bad men?" asked Alan. "He said he had business at the bank. Why didn't he get money from there?".

"I don't know why, Alan," answered Albert, "but he probably tried to but was refused and then went to Robb's. It's an expensive business moving house and then your Dad's got all the repairs to do and pay for. Perhaps that's why he needed the money," suggested Albert. "Next week your Dad will have to pay again! We can wait and see what happens then. If there's any more trouble you will have to tell your parents about me. That way I can help them," said Albert.

He knew there would be trouble. Just like he'd had. There was no reasoning with these men.

house and then your Dad's got all the repairs to do and pay for. Perhaps that's why he needed the money," suggested Albert. "Next week, your Dad will have to pay again! We can wait and see what happens then. If there's any more trouble you will have to tell your parents about me. That way I can help them," said Albert.

He knew there would be trouble. Just like he'd had. There was no reasoning with these men.

Chapter 7

The week passed very quickly. Mr Roper had worked hard and finished many parts of the house. It was starting to look transformed.

Today was Friday. The day Mr Roper had to pay money to the Robb's. He was not looking forward to the ordeal. He intended to have lunch and then go into Yanihill. He didn't get the chance.

Sid and Will Robb drove up to the house in their Mercedes.

"Sid, this is the house where we found that dead old man we ripped off," said Will feeling decidedly uncomfortable.

"Yes, and we never did get our money," said Sid annoyed.

The children, playing outside, watched as the

73

two men went to the front door. Mr Roper answered and stared in amazement at the men.

"How dare you come to my house," he said angrily.

"That must be the evil men," said Jodie. "Let's go and tell Albert and listen at the cellar door."

They ran round to the hatch and climbed in, taking Snoopy with them.

"Albert, those men are here," said Jodie putting on her locket and running up the stairs quietly.

"I was coming in to pay you later," said Mr Roper. "Now leave my house at once," he ordered.

"That's not very polite of you, Mr Roper. Is it, Sid?" said Will to his brother.

"We were in the neighbourhood and just thought we would save you a trip into Yanihill," said Sid, "so why don't you just give us our money," he added nicely.

"I don't have it yet," replied Mr Roper. "I have to go to the bank for it."

Mrs Roper came to the door to see what was happening.

"Go and put the kettle on," said Mr Roper, urging her to leave in case there was a scene.

"You have a pretty wife, Mr Roper, and lovely children. I do hope it stays that way," said Sid, threateningly.

"Don't threaten me, or my family," said Mr Roper angrily.

"Or what?" said Sid grabbing Mr Roper by the neck and shaking him.

"Or I'll get the police," replied Mr Roper croaking.

"They can't do anything to us. It's just you and us," said Will. "Perhaps Mr Roper needs a reminder of what happens to people who mess with us, Sid," said Will suggestively.

"Yes, I think he does," said Sid landing a punch on Mr Roper's jaw. He fell to the floor.

Jodie and Alan relayed what was going on to Albert.

"Let the dog out," ordered Albert as he turned to Snoopy and said, "get them boy, go and get them."

Alan opened the cellar door and let Snoopy out and then shut the door. Snoopy lunged at the men barking and growling and snarling.

"Oh, shut up you, stupid mutt," said Will kicking the dog.

Snoopy flew into the air squealing. He landed with a thud. Again he tried to attack the men and this time he was rewarded. He sank his teeth into Will's leg as hard as he could. He held on shaking and pulling at the flesh. Will, yelling, grabbed Snoopy by the tail and pulled him off sending him sliding along the floor. Mrs Roper came out of the kitchen.

"What on earth is going on here?" she demanded, as she saw her husband getting to his feet holding his burst lip.

"Don't get yourself involved in this, little lady," said Sid pinning her up against the wall "or I'll just have to re-arrange your face," he added viciously.

"Jeff, do something," she shouted, terrified.

Mr Roper was brawling with Will. Snoopy saw his chance to help Mrs Roper. He jumped in the air and bit Sid's bottom and clung on swinging to and fro, his teeth embedded deep in the flesh. Sid had to admit defeat and shouted to his brother.

"Will, get this mongrel off me."

Will held Snoopy by the back legs and pulled the dog away. Snoopy still determined to see them off, maintained his attack, snapping at their heals. Sid and Will gave in for now.

"Get the money to us today," said Sid nastily, clutching his bottom, "or we'll be back and next time your wife will need a plastic surgeon to fix her face." he added, slamming the door as he left.

"My goodness, what is happening to us?" cried Mrs Roper through her sobs. "I'm scared Jeff. They said they would hurt my face," she added trembling from head to foot. "I think I'm going to be sick," she mumbled running upstairs to the toilet. Mr Roper tried to pull himself together. He couldn't let his wife see that he too was scared.

Jodie and Alan came running in the front door.

"Dad, are you alright?" they asked.

"Did they hurt you?" Alan asked, seeing his father's lip was bleeding.

"Oh, it's just a scratch. It's nothing," he replied pretending that the situation wasn't serious.

"Where's Mum?" asked Jodie looking around.

"She's upstairs," he answered.

"Is she hurt?" Alan asked worried.

"No, she's fine," he reassured them.

"We – Jodie and I – need to talk to you both and it's very important, Dad," stated Alan feeling very grown up.

"Alright son, but not now, later," said Mr Roper concerned about his wife and going upstairs.

He had no idea just how vital Alan's information would be; if he believed it.

"But, Dad it's about those bad men," said Alan trying to make his dad listen.

"I'll be back in a few minutes," he insisted. Mrs Roper had been sick but was alright now though still very scared. "Come on pet, you have to be brave for the kids' sake," he urged gently.

"I know," she said and blew her nose. "That's better, now let's see to Alan and Jodie."

"Now then young man, what did you want to tell us?" asked Mr Roper coming downstairs with his wife.

"We have a friend," Alan began, "and he told us that those bad men had lent him money too, and he got into a lot of trouble," he went on.

"He wants to help you," said Jodie.

"What friend is this?" asked Mr Roper doubting them as he knew they hadn't been anywhere to make new friends.

"He's Uncle Albert," Jodie replied. "He lives in the cellar, well he doesn't really live, as he's dead.

He's a ghost," she stated proudly. None of her friends had ever had a ghost as a friend.

"Stop this, both of you. It's not helping. I've never heard such nonsense. There is no such thing as ghosts," declared Mr Roper.

"Yes there is, Dad! Uncle Albert is real," said Alan.

"He is real and look he gave me this to keep," said Jodie taking the locket from her pocket.

"And he gave me this," said Alan showing them the ring. "Before we could only hear Albert but after he gave us these gifts we can see him as well," he informed them.

"I've heard enough," stated Mr Roper. "You had no right to be in the cellar and go into those boxes. That's stealing. Give those to your mother now and don't go into the cellar again. Is that understood?"

"Yes, Dad." They lied. They had to go and see Albert. He was the only one that could help them.

"Go out and play, or better still, go for a ride on your bikes and use up some of your energy," said Mrs Roper taking the jewellery from them.

Jodie and Alan immediately disobeyed their father, went straight to the hatch and into the cellar.

They had to talk to Albert .

"Albert, Uncle Albert," said Jodie forgetting that she didn't have her locket.

"Quick Jodie, help me with the box and we'll get something else so we can hear him," suggested Alan. They took out a string of beads each and put them on, Alan feeling a little stupid wearing a necklace but this was too important for it to bother him too much.

They told Albert everything that had happened.

"We told Mum and Dad about you but they didn't believe us," said Alan sadly.

"You will just have to keep at them until they do believe you. I am going to need their help," said Albert, his voice coming from the chair.

"Have you thought of a plan yet?" asked Jodie.

"Yes, I have," he replied. "Do you have bicycles?"

"Yes, we do," they answered, wanting to hear his plan.

"Good, because I want you to deliver a letter to the Robb's office," said Albert.

"But it will be dangerous," said Alan, "and Dad would kill us for being so stupid."

"Don't worry," said Albert. "All you have to do is wait until your father is in the office. The men will take him through to another room. While he's in there you can slip the envelope under the door. If it does look dangerous then tell a passer-by that you found the letter and could they hand it in for you. Have you got that?" asked Albert seeing the relief on their faces at his alternative suggestion.

"What does the letter say, Uncle Albert?" asked Jodie.

"It's grown up stuff kiddo, but it should start my plan off very well," he reassured them.

Alan took the letter and folding it, he put it in his back pocket.

"What is the office called and where is it?" asked Alan.

"It's called Fastcash and it's–"

"I saw it, I know where it is," interrupted Jodie, cutting Albert off in mid sentence.

"Right then, off you go and be careful," said Albert. "Good luck!"

Jodie and Alan felt very important, like secret agents. They took off the beads, hiding them under the chair and then left the cellar.

Chapter 8

"Mum, can we ride into town on our bikes?" asked Alan.

"Only if you promise to go past the Post Office. You could also get me some milk while you're there," she added "but you can have your lunch first. Sit down and I'll bring it over."

"I'll get the milk for you, dear," offered Mr Roper.

The children had their lunch and left, safe in the knowledge that Mr Roper would be close behind them. He was going to Fastcash. What he didn't know was that Albert was in the car with him. Jodie and Alan reached Yanihill before their dad. He passed them on Main Street and waved.

They waited at the Post Office and watched him

crossing the road and going to the bank. They hid up a side street nearer Fastcash. They then saw dad enter the office. Albert followed him.

"It's time to make our move," said Alan cycling across the road.

They dropped their bikes in front of the shop next door. Slowly, peeking in the window they saw no one was in the front office. Alan made a dash for it and slipped the letter under the door.

"Quick Jodie, let's get out of here before we get caught," said Alan looking triumphantly at Jodie. "This is fun," he said picking up his bike.

They rode like the clappers to get as far away as they could, so their dad would think they had gone to the Post Office and turned back straight away, like they had been told.

Mr Roper came out of the small office and saw a man put a letter on the desk as he left.

Will noticed the letter.

"Is this from you?" he asked the man waiting.

"No, I found it on the floor when I came in," the man replied.

"Please excuse me for a minute," said Will walking into the small office. He opened the letter

84

and it read;

> Beware you wretched villains,
>
> Take heed of what I say,
>
> The swinging man will seek revenge,
>
> To make sure that you pay.
>
> I'm the secret you always kept,
>
> You wronged me then, as well,
>
> So I have risen out my grave,
>
> To send you both to hell!
>
> The Swinging Man

"What in heavens name is this?" said Will handing the letter to Sid.

"It's anonymous, Will. It's signed 'The Swinging Man'."

"What does it mean?" asked Will unnerved.

"I guess it must be a customer of ours who has died and a relative is trying to get back at us. Well, it didn't work. I'm not scared," said Sid scrunching the letter up and throwing it onto the desk.

"Oh, you're not scared," thought Albert. "Maybe this will help then," he chuckled to himself.

Albert blew on the ball of paper. It rolled off the desk. Sid and Will stared at it in disbelief. Albert blew again and made it roll over the carpet and round the room. Will was terrified. He jumped onto the chair and kept watching the paper.

"What's going on? Who's doing that?" he asked.

Sid looked round the room. "There isn't a window open, so it can't be a draught," he said starting to feel uneasy.

Albert blew on all the papers on the desk. Everything went flying about and floated to the floor.

"Maybe it was a small earthquake," said Sid clutching at straws for an explanation.

"Explain this," thought Albert. He lifted up the table lamp and waved it about.

"A floating lamp," thought Will unable to speak. He just pointed at it. Albert then lifted the telephone receiver and made it snake it's way through the air, up and down. Sid was rooted to the spot, his mouth hanging open, terrified.

"It's some kind of supernatural force," Sid squeaked. To put the icing on the cake, Albert spun the swivel chair that Will was standing on. He burled round and flew off, landing on the floor.

"Ahh! Ahh! Ahh!" he yelled, fleeing from the

86

offices in terror. He was closely followed by Sid, who grabbed the man in the outer office and threw him out saying they were closed.

Albert left, laughing hysterically. "What a spectacle," he thought. "It was worth waiting for."

Back at the house everything had settled down. Jodie and Alan, finding Albert gone, waited for his return. They laughed themselves silly when Albert told them the story.

"It serves them right for what they did to you and to our Mum and Dad," said Jodie.

"I wish I had seen it," said Alan, still chuckling.

"I will have to write another letter," said Albert. "I'll drive them out of town if it's the last thing I do."

"Yes, good riddance to bad rubbish," said Alan. They talked about the plan until it was time for dinner.

"We'll see you tomorrow, Albert, or rather we'll hear you tomorrow," said Jodie.

"That reminds me, the beads are a gift," said Albert. That meant the children could really see him. "Bye," he added.

After dinner the children watched a film on television, glad that dad had stopped hammering and they had peace to watch it. Nothing left worth watching, they went to bed.

Mr and Mrs Roper followed shortly. Mr Roper lay snoring softly but Mrs Roper couldn't sleep. She tossed and turned, worried about the Robb's coming back to the house.

"What are we going to do about the money?" she asked herself totally desperate. She didn't know where to turn. She found herself thinking about Uncle Albert and the more she thought about it she realised the children did seem to make so much sense. She wanted to believe them. "The kids aren't liars," she thought. They knew too much to be making it up.

Before she realised what she was doing curiosity had got the better of her. She got out of bed and put her dressing gown on. "There's only one way to find out if there really is an Uncle Albert. Now, what was it the children said about hearing him?" she asked herself. "Ah, yes, the locket. I've got to wear something," she thought taking the locket from her trinket box where she had put it for safekeeping. "If Jeff wakens he'll probably think I've gone for a drink. That will give me a little time," she thought.

She tiptoed out the bedroom and crept down

the stairs. She got to the cellar door and reached out for the handle. Her hand was shaking like a leaf. Her whole body was trembling. She was terrified.

"Oh, Anna, you are being ridiculous," she chided herself and opened the door quickly. She put the light on and crept down the stairs feeling like her legs could give way at any moment. She put the locket on and whispered, "Hello?"

Nothing.

"Hello, is anyone here?" she asked, her throat dry. She swallowed hard and went on, "I hope I'm not disturbing you. My children said it would be alright if I came to see you."

Still nothing

"I know it's late," she went on, moving further into the cellar, "but it took me a while to pluck up the courage to come down here. You see I don't believe in ghosts but I know my children aren't liars and wouldn't make this up," she confessed. "What am I saying? What am I doing here? I must be mad!" she stated out loud and turned to go back upstairs.

She got to the first step and "Stay," came a voice from the far corner of the room. Mrs Roper just about collapsed with shock. She grabbed the banister, to steady herself.

"Please stay," came the voice again.

Mrs Roper turned her head slowly and stared in the direction of the voice. She thought she was crazy. "Could this be true? Is this real or am I just hearing things?" she asked herself. She wasn't going to wait around and find out the answers to her questions. Her knees were knocking together. In blind panic and like a woman possessed, Mrs Roper fled from the cellar on rubber legs taking the stairs two at a time until she reached the safety of her bedroom. She bounced onto the bed and started beating Mr Roper on the chest.

"Wake up Jeff, wake up," she wailed.

"What's going on?" he mumbled, half asleep.

"Wake up now," she begged.

Realising there was something wrong, Mr Roper sat bolt upright in bed now fully awake.

"Calm down, Anna," he said staring at his wife who was as white as a sheet. "You look as if you have seen a ghost," he said.

"I have, I have, well not really, but I heard it, Jeff. I heard it. I really did. You have to believe me," she ranted.

"Slow down Anna, slow down," he said soothingly. "It's alright you're safe now I'm here. You've just had a bad dream," he said holding her lightly in his arms.

"No Jeff, it wasn't a dream, really it wasn't," she protested. "I went to the cellar. I found myself believing the children; they knew too much. I went to the cellar and he spoke, this man, ghost, Albert or whatever. He did Jeff, he did. He said 'stay', 'please stay'. I was so scared I ran up here as fast as I could. Come with me, please? You have to believe me," she pleaded.

"Okay, okay," said Mr Roper. "So what you are saying is the kids are telling the truth! They didn't make this up? There is a ghost called Albert in the cellar?" he asked in disbelief.

"Yes Jeff, it's true, it's really true. Come with me and we'll go and see him," said Mrs Roper.

Mr Roper put on his robe and slippers, thinking to himself that he had better humour his wife or he wouldn't get back to sleep. He didn't believe her!

"Here, here," said Mrs Roper handing her husband the silver ring.

"Oh right, I need this to hear don't I?" he said leaving the bedroom.

Again Mrs Roper entered the cellar. This time not so afraid, because her husband was with her. "Hello, Albert are you there?" she asked.

There was no reply. "Please Mr-er-, Albert talk to us," she pleaded, wanting to convince Mr Roper she was for real. "I'm sorry I ran away but you scared me," she went on. "My husband is here now. Like me he doesn't believe in ghosts, but *I* do now."

"Hello," came the voice from the corner. Mr Roper standing on the last step stumbled, his legs giving way, and fell to the floor. "I'm sorry, I seem to frighten people easily these days," said Albert.

Mr Roper was in shock. He couldn't speak. He couldn't believe this was happening. "Ghosts, ghosts," he thought to himself. "I've seen films with ghosts but there's just no way I ever took them seriously," he thought getting to his feet.

"Er, er, is it true that you are friends with my – our children?" asked Mr Roper.

"Yes, it's true and they are wonderful children," said Albert, proud to know them.

"I'm sorry, we didn't believe them."

"That's alright," said Albert. "Not many people would. You need my help, don't you?" he asked.

"Yes if you wouldn't –," answered Mrs Roper.

"All in good time," replied Albert. "Do you realise just how much trouble you are in?" he asked.

"What do you mean?" asked Mr Roper.

"It's simple. You made an agreement with these evil men and they won't stop until they have every penny you own or can borrow," stated Albert. "I should know," he added. "I have a plan and its already started but I have to keep it going if it's to work."

"Tell us what we have to do," said Mrs Roper desperate to end the nightmare.

"I need you to take me to Fastcash tomorrow to deliver a letter. I will remain there to see what happens. Is that alright?" asked Albert.

"Of course," answered Mr Roper. "Anything," he added.

"You can bring me back, it's a long walk for an old man and after doing it today, I'm bushed," he said.

"You were there today?" asked Mr Roper.

"Yes, I was in your car and I was with you the whole time," answered Albert.

He explained what had gone on that day and

assured him that his children were never in danger. "I have to keep the pressure on and then finish it off for good," said Albert. "I've got them scared witless and it's only going to get worse for them," added Albert. "Then they will walk into my trap," he finished. They all talked 'till the early hours of the morning.

Chapter 9

Later that morning the children rose to a celebratory breakfast. Their parents explained what had happened the previous night and then apologised.

"We knew you wouldn't believe us," said Jodie.

"But we had to try to make you somehow," added Alan.

"I'm just so pleased that we will have Albert helping us," said Mrs Roper.

Mr Roper was still wearing the ring and his wife the locket. The mood was happy in the house. No more secrets and no more lies.

"When you're finished eating, can you go and ask Albert what time he wants to go to Fastcash?" asked Mr Roper. "We have got another letter to deliver," he added.

The kids obliged and came back with the reply, "He says he is ready when you are."

"Can we come?" asked the kids, pleading with him.

"Yes, your Mum's coming too but you have to stay in the car."

A letter floated through the air and into Alan's hand.

"Wow!" said Mr Roper.

"Good morning," said Albert. Alan handed Jodie her beads; he was already wearing his.

An hour later they all left in the car for Yanihill and the to visit Fastcash. This time Mr Roper would deliver the letter and if the coast wasn't clear he would give it to someone so it couldn't be traced back to them.

Whey they got there the office was closed.

"You must have spooked them good," said Mr Roper.

"Yes, it's worked but these villains are too greedy to stay closed when they could be robbing someone else –'Robb by name and rob by nature' – that's them," stated Albert.

"Look, there they are now," said Mr Roper.

"You were right Albert," he added.

"I've got a better idea," said Albert. "Watch this."

Taking the letter from Alan, he got out of the car. The letter flew about as if blown by the wind. Up and down it fluttered and then flew past the men and under the door. Will looked about like a frightened rabbit. Sid looked up to the sky and turned around checking but there wasn't anything behind him.

"This is giving me the creeps," said Will as Sid opened the door.

"It might just have been the wind and we don't know if the letter is for us," said Sid hoping he was right.

He picked up the letter and turned it over.

"The Robbers, it says. I guess it is for us," said Sid shaking in his shoes.

"Read it then," said Will.

> You found me then you fled the scene,
> Knowing you were to blame,
> I know now that you're cowards,
> and you ran to hide your shame,
> Now you must know who I am,
> and believe it for it's true,

For I just cannot rest in peace
It's "Payback Time" for you.

I've come back to haunt you,
Open your ears and you will hear,
I'm the swinging man,
It's me you have to fear.

The Swinging Man

Both men stared at each other.

"This can't be ha-ha-happening," stammered Will realising who the letters had been from.

"There's no such thing as ghosts – only in movies," stated Sid.

"Oh, is that right," said Albert to himself. "We will just have to see about that," he added, thinking of phase two of his plan.

"We can't let this get to us, Will," said Sid trying to come to terms with what was going on.

A punch came from nowhere and landed on Sid's nose. He fired into the desk backwards.

"Crikey! I'm out of here!" yelled Will fleeing out the door. Sid sorted himself. The punch hadn't been too hard. Albert was an old ghost after all.

Sid ran after Will and caught him. "Pull yourself together, man," he ordered.

"I can't Sid, I'm scared. There's a ghost after us. What are we going to do?" he asked shaking uncontrollably.

"Look, I'm scared too but maybe if we play along and be nice, he might go away," suggested Sid.

"I don't want to find out," whimpered Will.

"We have money to collect today so get your act together and get back into the office," Sid demanded, walking away. Will followed reluctantly.

The family watched from the car. Jodie and Alan were laughing at the men. Mrs Roper laughed too, remembering how terrified she had been.

"Those men must be terrified," she said. "I know I was and Albert is our friend and he was nice to us but those men are in for a very rough ride."

"Albert could drive them crazy," said Mr Roper. "It's no better than what they deserve."

Sid opened the office door and Albert slammed it shut in his face.

"Oh God! Please. I'm sorry, I'm sorry. What can we do? We'll do anything," begged Sid his legs going numb.

He tried the door again and went in. Albert left, laughing as the two men stared about them petrified, not knowing what was coming next.

Albert got in the car. Everyone was still roaring with laughter.

"Nice one, Albert," said Mr Roper. "You've really got them worried," he added.

"I know," replied Albert, "but I have to take it a stage further and I need your help for that."

"Sure thing. What do you want me to do?" asked Mr Roper.

"It's asking a lot I know, but I need you to pretend you don't have the money when you are due to pay them next," stated Albert. "I will give you a box of war medals you can offer them. They are very valuable and I'm sure they will accept them instead of money."

"Yes, I can do that, but why?" Mr Roper asked, worried about getting another beating.

"Once they have accepted them, the medals are their property and they will be able to hear me then," explained Albert.

"Brilliant," said Mr Roper understanding his plan and not caring if he did get a beating. It would be worth it. They drove home planning their next move. "By the way, you can keep the beads," said Albert as he suddenly became visible to Mr and Mrs Roper.

"Wow!" said Jeff looking in the rear view mirror. "Hi there. It's nice to see you."

Chapter 10

The next few days were a lot of fun. Albert was part of the family now and he only went back to the cellar when everyone went to bed.

They had all gone for a picnic on the other side of Yanihill. They had pitched the rugs on the riverbank near the railway line. It had been a beautiful day and the children had watched a freight train with fifty-four crates go over the level crossing. They had spotted a beautiful house all on its own up on a hillside. Albert told them that it belonged to Sid and Will Robb. The kids wondered just how many people they had ripped off to afford a house like that.

They had all gone to the ice rink and got wet bottoms falling on the ice. Jodie was the only one that was a competent skater. But they had all had fun.

They sat up very late and played cards. Mr Roper enjoying the time spent away from fixing the house.

Yet again, Friday was upon them. Mr Roper and the family all went to Fastcash. Mr Roper and Albert went in. They were taken into the small office.

"I don't want any trouble," began Mr Roper, "but I don't have the money."

"Oh! you don't want any trouble," sniggered Will looking at Sid.

"I've got these instead. They are very valuable. They are worth more than what I owe you in full."

"And just what are they?" asked Will taking the box from Mr Roper. "Well, lookie here!" said Will staring wide eyed into the box.

"They were my grandfather's," Mr Roper lied.

Sid looked at them unimpressed. "Why they're just some old bits of tin he got for being a brave boy," stated Sid pushing the box away in disgust. "No, we want cash," he demanded.

"Excuse us a minute," said Will beckoning Sid out into the front office. "Are you mad or just stupid?" asked Will. "These are worth a small fortune."

"Who's going to buy them from us, clever clogs?" asked Sid.

"In a few weeks that military lot are coming again and the place will be swarming with buyers. We can make a killing on these. Now, shut up and let me do the talking," Will ordered.

"I think we can come to an arrangement," said Will. "These should cover two weeks money," he stated flatly.

"Two weeks money!" exclaimed Mr Roper. "That's not a fair deal."

"We are not here to be fair, Mr Roper. This is not a pawnbrokers or a secondhand shop. It is a business. Now take it or leave it," said Will. "You know what will happen if you don't! Such a pretty wife, really pretty," he threatened.

"Alright, it's a deal," agreed Mr Roper, secretly delighted. Now Albert could really put on the pressure.

Sid marked Mr Roper's card and he left with Albert and went back to the car. Albert told them of his plan and went back to the office, while the Ropers waited for him in the car.

The men were debating how much each medal could be worth.

Albert went right up to Will's ear and said,

"Boo," very loudly. Will jumped six feet in the air.

"Ahh! it's back again. I can hear it," he yelled.

"I heard it too," said Sid frozen to the spot.

"Get away from us. Leave us alone," begged Will.

Again Albert went to his ear and said, "No."

"Ahh," wailed Will bolting for the door.

Albert barred the door. Will wrestled with the handle and pulled for all he was worth to get the door open.

"Oh no, you don't," said Albert.

"Ahh!" he yelled again, jumping back from the door and running to shield himself behind the desk. Sid was frantic.

"What do you want from us?" he asked staring round the room looking for clues as to Albert's whereabouts.

"Up here boys!" said Albert swinging from the light fitting. "Over here," he went on, spinning the swivel chair round. The filing cabinet drawers started to open and close and open and close. Albert grabbed files and threw them into the air, paper flying everywhere.

Albert flung the telephone at Sid. "Ouch!" he

cried as it hit his head. The room was in an uproar. Everything that wasn't nailed down Albert lifted and flung at the men.

"Help! help us," screamed Will out of his mind with fear, dodging the waste paper bin.

"Ouch!" cried Sid as the table lamp hit him on the head, the bulb smashed and showered him in glass.

"Bullseye," shouted Albert triumphantly.

"He's out to get us," wailed Sid.

"Yes, I am," replied Albert, switching on the paper shredder.

"Oh crikey, run for it," shouted Will visualising his hand like a half pound of ground beef. He made a quick getaway screaming all the way.

Sid was close behind with the medals tucked under his arm. Albert noticed a cigar lighter that had been knocked off the desk in all the excitement. He picked it up and set light to the papers on the floor.

The Ropers watched eagerly and saw the two men running from the shop in blind panic. Watching for Albert coming, they could see flames leaping high into the air in the small office as he left the building.

"Wow! look at that!" exclaimed Alan. "That's

going to be some bonfire."

Albert got into the car and told them what he had done. None of the other shops were in any danger. Albert wouldn't have risked that. "I won't stop until these evil men have nothing. Then they will know what it is like to go to a bank and be refused and turn to someone else for help, only to find that they stab you in the back and rob you at every turn," he stated.

"That's if you don't run them out of town first," said Mrs Roper, giggling at the thought.

"What are you going to do now?" Jodie asked Albert, watching the flames engulf the front office.

"I'm going to go to their house and spook them some more," answered Albert. "Can you give me a lift? It's just up the road," asked Albert, looking at Jeff.

"Yes, let's go," he said starting the car.

Hearing the fire sirens he said, "Just drop me here." He got out at the level crossing. "I'll be back later," he added walking towards the Robb's house.

The doorbell rang.

"Who the devil can that be?" asked Will going to the door. He opened it and 'thud' as a punch landed on him. He staggered backwards, his legs doing their best to keep him on his feet.

"No!" screamed Will. "No, he's here Sid. He knows where we live," he wailed, running off to hide.

Albert found him crouched down behind a chair in the lounge. "Boo," said Albert, rolling the chair over.

"Ahh! Sid, help me," screamed Will frightened out of his wits, running round the room like a headless chicken.

Sid came into the room. "Please Mr – er –, tell us what you want. We'll do anything," Sid pleaded.

"I want my life," boomed Albert into Sid's face.

"I-I-I don't understand," replied Sid.

"You took it!" shouted Albert into Will's ear.

"Ahh," cried Will running out the room.

"Give it back," demanded Albert.

"But, but I-I," stuttered Sid.

"No, you can't, can you?" stated Albert moving round the room.

"N-n-no," replied Sid.

"You didn't give me a chance. You hounded me for money. You took everything I had so now it's payback time."

"If it's money you want, I can give you money."

"I don't want money!" yelled Albert. "I want you to suffer. I won't rest until you have nothing. Just like all the poor people that come to you for help."

The coffee table flew into the air and crashed down onto the fireplace. Sid ducked as a flying clock barely missed him. Photographs, ornaments, everything that could be used as a missile was launched into mid air. The lounge was totally ransacked. Nothing was left standing.

"Now at least nobody will come to you for a loan," said Albert.

"What do you mean?" asked Sid frightened to move.

"You don't have an office. It's a burned out shell," laughed Albert heading for the door. "I'll be back," he said, slamming the door so hard the glass shattered.

"Will, get yourself in here. He's gone," shouted Sid.

Will stared in shock at the mess in the lounge. It looked as if a bomb had hit it.

"Why didn't you run and hide?" asked Will still shaking.

"I was too scared to move," replied Sid.

"What are we going to do?" asked Will.

"I don't know," said Sid, "but we have got other problems. That lunatic ghost has burnt down the office. We'll have to go round and collect everyone's money from now on," he added his fear gone and anger setting in. "We'll have to up the rates to cover our loss of the shop," he added angrily.

"Is that all you can think about – money?" asked Will. "Don't you see, if he's already burned down the office, he could burn down the house and we'd be left with nothing."

"That's what he wants, Will," said Sid. "He wants us to have nothing," he finished.

"We're ruined, we're doomed!" said Will.

Chapter 11

Albert made it home. He told the Ropers the whole story and they planned phase three.

"This should do it once and for all. Anna, I need you to make a replica of Jeff and I," said Albert.

"No problem," said Mrs Roper going off to get her sewing basket.

"The kids can make papier-maché heads. It doesn't have to look like us too much," he added.

"We've got wigs and everything for dressing up," said Jodie excitedly.

Albert and Mr Roper put the saw bench back in the cellar and Mr Roper got some lengths of rope.

Anna and the children took a couple of days to finish the dummies. Everything was ready now. The trap was set. This time the men were in for a surprise.

Sid and Will drove round daily collecting their money. They were more vicious than before. They had to get as much money as possible so they could buy a new office in another town. They were going to sell their house and move on, they couldn't live there anymore as the ghost would keep coming back to destroy everything they had.

Will couldn't take much more. He was a bully, but underneath, like most bullies, he was a coward. But, every day that the ghost didn't spook them, Will was getting braver.

Albert decided to pay the brothers a visit before they came to the Ropers' house the next day. It would frighten them afresh and warm things up. He waited until evening. Sid and Will were in their beds asleep. Albert went into a bedroom and saw Will asleep. He took hold of the footboard on the bed and started shaking it violently. Will woke up.

"Blimey, an earthquake," he said out loud as he wobbled about on the bed and switched the light on.

Albert stopped. Will looked about the room. Satisfied that what he thought was an earthquake was over, he put the light off to go back to sleep. Albert switched the light back on.

"Now the power is on the blink," said Will still not realising it was Albert. He put the light off. It went on. He put it off. It went on. Will sat up looking about. He broke out in a cold sweat, his heart started pounding, his blood was racing, knowing now it hadn't been an earthquake. It was him; the ghost.

Suddenly Albert went round the room like a tornado. Will sat shaking, clutching his duvet as he watched his books fly from his bookshelf. His clothes danced out of the wardrobe and fell in a heap on the floor. The pictures on the wall were swinging. His socks and pants exploded out of the drawers, then came his shirts, like waltzing torsos.

"Leave me alone, please," whimpered Will.

"Why should I?" boomed the voice in his face.

"Help!" cried Will tearing out of the room and into Sid's. "Sid, wake up! Wake up!" he screamed.

Sid opened his eyes and rubbed them. "What is it, Will?" he asked, half asleep.

"It's him, he's here again," squeaked Will. "He's trashing my bedroom."

Sid could hear the crashing and banging. Then it stopped. They both sat motionless staring at the door. Nothing happened. Ten minutes passed, with-

115

out incident. They both still sat there, their heartbeats returning to normal, thinking the ghost had gone. Then suddenly without warning Albert burst into Sid's bedroom with an axe over his head. Albert let out an almighty scream, "Aaaahhh!" as he brought the axe down on the bed.

"Aaaahhh!" screamed Sid and Will leaping off the bed and racing downstairs.

"Let's leave now and get out of here," begged Will crying with fear. Sid grabbed the car keys.

"Come on," said Sid as they ran out the house like mad men.

They drove like the bats out of hell but as they crossed the level crossing the car came to an abrupt halt.

"What's wrong?" asked Will.

"I don't know. The accelerator is stuck."

The barriers came down and the ground shook as the night train approached. It sounded its horn. Sid and Will tried to get out but the doors were locked.

"Oh no, it's the ghost!" said Sid.

"Put your foot down, try, try!" screamed Will.

"I am, it won't work," said Sid frantically.

They clawed and scratched at the door handles,

trying to get out. The train got nearer and nearer, it's lights shining in the car windows.

"Oh we're going to die, we're going to die," yelled Sid.

As the train was about to hit them the tyres screeched as the accelerator hit the floor. Dirt and dust flew up as the car sped away only seconds from being crushed by the train. It skidded out of control and finally came to a stop.

Sid and Will were crying.

"He nearly killed us," said Sid trying to pull himself together.

"He could try again at any time," said Will. "We need to leave here now."

"We can't," said Sid. "We have to sell the house first. It will only take a couple of weeks. We can try and reason with the ghost if he comes back."

Too scared to go back to the house, the men drove to a quiet spot and slept in the car.

Albert was waiting for the Ropers to get up; he wanted to recount the story of last night. He now felt sure that the men would leave for good after last night and the performance that was waiting for them later that day.

If everything went to plan it would be a success.

The family rose and ate. Everyone was excited about today.

"Don't forget we have some finishing touches to do downstairs," said Albert looking at Mr Roper.

"We should really get to it now," said Mr Roper. "We don't know what time our guests will be stopping by," he said, laughing.

Albert and Mr Roper went to the cellar and hung up the dummy with a large thick rope round its neck, tying it to the beam on the cellar's ceiling. They plugged in the saw.

"Where's the red food dye?" asked Albert.

"I forgot it, it's upstairs. I'll get it."

"Anna, where's the red food dye?" asked Mr Roper.

"Catch," said Mrs Roper as she tossed it to him. "Oh, wouldn't you be better mixing it with a little ketchup?" she suggested. "It will look more realistic, it will look like blood then."

"We'll give it a try," said Mr Roper.

Albert and Jeff cut off the head from Jeff's dummy and put the blood mixture on the neck and round the collar of the body. They put the head on the floor at the end of the saw bench and put plenty of blood around it. Mr Roper put the blood stuff on his fingers, flicking them at the wall making it look as if it had been sprayed there when Jeff's head had been cut off. They put the blood on the saw blade and left Jeff's dummy slumped over the end of the saw bench.

"Anna, come and see this," called Mr Roper to his wife.

The children and Mrs Roper went to see. "Eeh, yuck!" said Mrs Roper. "That looks gruesome."

"It looks brill," said Alan.

"Yes, it does," agreed Jodie.

Mr Roper got one of the large cardboard boxes and wet the bottom with water and left a puddle on the floor. He added the mixture and swirled it about. "Leave a shoe beside the box and then they'll think that the children are in the box," Albert suggested.

"Jodie," called Mr Roper. "Bring me one of your shoes and Alan's catapult."

Jodie gave him the shoe and the catapult. "Are Alan and I supposed to be in that box?" she asked.

"Yes," said Mr Roper.

"Oh goodie," she exclaimed, excited that although she wouldn't be there when the men came, she still had a part to play.

The box in place, Mr Roper changed the light bulb for a dimmer one. The men would find it hard to see and they wouldn't realise that the bodies were only dummies. Everything was ready. Albert got two of Mary's hair pins and put them beside the saw.

They waited impatiently for the men to arrive.

"They're taking forever," said Alan fed up that the show hadn't begun.

"Battle stations, everyone," said Mr Roper. "I can hear a car."

Mrs Roper, the children and Snoopy ran upstairs and hid inside their wardrobes as instructed. Mr Roper opened the front door a little. He opened the cellar door, put the light on and went down. Albert put the saw on and Jeff climbed out the hatch and spied on the men.

They had reached the front door. Jeff gave the signal and Albert switched off the saw. Jeff pushed the log bunker in front of the hatch; they had nowhere to run.

"Mr Roper, Mr Roper are you down there?"

"He must be. I heard a saw," said Will. "He just

hasn't heard us," he said, heading down the cellar stairs.

Sid followed him. Mr Roper crept over to the cellar door and silently closed and then bolted it. "Yes!" he thought "they're trapped."

"Hello, Mr Roper we've come for our money," said Sid wondering why Mr Roper wouldn't answer.

One by one, Will and Sid crept down the stairs. "I don't like this, Sid," said Will. "This is where we found the dead man. It's creepy in here. I can't see very much it's so dark."

Albert floated into the air and entered the dummy. "Hello," said the voice.

"Mr – Mr Roper is that you?" asked Sid starting to get scared. They walked further into the cellar.

"Mr Roper," said Sid again.

"It's me," came Albert's voice from the ceiling.

"Good God," exclaimed Sid staring at the hanging man.

"He is a ghost," whimpered Will paralysed on the spot.

"I'm the Swinging Man," said Albert.

"We c-c-came t-to see Mr Roper," stuttered Sid.

"Who is Mr Roper?" asked Albert.

"He lives h-h-here," replied Sid.

"Do you mean him?" laughed Albert pointing to the dummy slumped over the saw bench.

"Run, run," said Sid making for the stairs. Sid ran up the stairs. Will stumbled and fell smacking his face off the step. Sid pulled and hauled at the door but it wouldn't open.

"We're locked in, Will," yelled Sid. Will tried the door but it was locked. Desperately, the men kicked at the door. Albert left the dummy.

"Here's a little present from me," said Albert taking Mary's hair pins and attached them to Sid and Will's jumpers. Standing at the bottom of the stairs Albert said, "There's no escape, boys. You just have to face up to it. It's payback time."

"There's two of them," cried Sid.

"Please, please," screeched Will. "We'll do anything. You can have our house and all our money."

"No, no, no!" said Albert. "You robbed the poor, you bled them dry. Revenge is sweet, it's time to die!"

Albert picked up the catapult and opened the jars of mouldy pickled onions.

"Look boys, these are the rotten eyeballs of some of my other victims," he said and roared with laughter. He pelted them with a barrage of onions.

"Ahh!" wailed Will, "Get them off me," he cried as he dodged about trying to avoid them.

Sid was screaming, tears running down his cheeks. They had never been so scared in their lives. Over and over they tried the door to no avail. The onion supply depleted, Albert took the pins off the men so they couldn't see him any more. Everything went quiet. Both men looked pitiful standing at the door sobbing, eyes wide in terror.

"Where's he gone?" asked Sid sniffing.

"I'm here," said Albert. "Now I'm here," as he moved about the room. They saw the shoe float in the air and get tossed into the box.

"Oh! he's killed the kids as well. We're dead, Sid. He's going to kill us!" cried Will.

Albert started up the saw.

Sid and Will kicked and kicked at the door. Screaming, wailing and crying; they were wrecks, out of their minds with fear.

"Who's first?" Albert asked. He took Will by the sleeve and started to drag him down the stairs.

"No, no h-elp! help me!" screamed Will. Sid watched as his brother got further away step by step.

"No, stop please, please," cried Sid. "Will! Oh, Will," he yelled still trying to break the door down.

Will was writhing about and fighting like a wild cat. Albert got him to within six feet of the saw. Albert reached out and switched the saw off.Mr Roper waiting for his cue, unbolted the door and stood behind it.

Albert let go of Will, who ran up the stairs screaming and yelling. Sid tried the door again and to his relief it opened. They ran out the cellar, out of the house and into the car.

Albert followed them in Mr Roper's car. Sid and Will were driving like mad men. They hurtled down the long driveway to get to the main road. Albert peeped his horn and drove right up behind them.

"He's after us," yelled Will. "Faster, go faster."

They veered off the dirt track and left skid marks on the tarmac they were going so fast.

"Bye, bye!" said Albert to himself as he stopped at the main road.

Chapter 12

Albert drove back to the house. The family was waiting on the steps for him.

"Well done, my man," said Mr Roper.

"It's over," said Albert sadly. "I had to scare them, they had to feel fear. I had to push them to their limit, just like they pushed me to mine and then over it. You see, I killed myself because of them."

"Is that your unfinished business finished?" asked Jodie.

"I think so," said Albert.

Suddenly, without warning beautiful bright white lights, like sparkling bubbles descended upon Albert.

"What's happening?" asked Jodie amazed.

"I think it's time for Albert to leave," said Mrs

Roper with hot tears running down her cheeks.

"I don't want you to leave," said Jodie, starting to cry.

"Neither do I," said Alan.

"He has to," said Mr Roper.

There was a dazzling flash of light and Albert was gone. Snoopy barked.

The next morning at breakfast everything was quiet. The house felt empty without Albert.

"I'll miss him," said Alan. They all agreed.

Snoopy sauntered in with the paper. "Thanks boy!" said Mr Roper patting him on the head. Mr Roper looked at the paper. The front page headlines read,

Loss of life as train takes out two men

Yesterday, in the local town of Yanihill, two men, described by eye witnesses, to be driving like crazed lunatics, ignored the level crossing barriers and were struck by a speeding freight train. They were later named as brothers, Sidney and William Robb.

We hope you have enjoyed this series of Shivers. In this series, there are six titles to collect.

Rag & Bone Man
Payback Time
Cold Kisser
Noisy Neighbours
Pen Pals
The Sold Souls

This series was concieved by Edgar J. Hyde and much of the text was provided by his minions, under slavish conditions and pain of death! Thankfully, none of these minions defied their master and so we can say 'thank you' to them for toughing it out and making this series possible.

Edgar J. Hyde, however, has yet more plans for these dungeon-bound slaves. 'No rest for the wicked' is his motto!